Seducing Sophia

Cameron Hart

Published by Cameron Hart, 2023.

This is a work of fiction. Similarities to real people, places, or events are entirely coincidental.

SEDUCING SOPHIA

First edition. September 5, 2023.

Copyright © 2023 Cameron Hart.

ISBN: 979-8227623652

Written by Cameron Hart.

Chapter 1

Aiden

"It's escalating," Logan, my agent, says, stating the obvious.

We stare at my vandalized car in silence, assessing the damage. The tires are slashed, the driver's side window is smashed in, and there's a note on the front seat. It's just a sheet of paper with letters cut out of a magazine – a little cliché, but still effective in the creepiness department. The note simply says *soon*.

I sigh and rub my eyes, hoping there will somehow be a set change by the time I open them. No such luck; this isn't a movie. This is my life, which now includes a crazy as fuck stalker.

"What else can we do?" I ask for what feels like the tenth time. It's not the first run in I've had with overzealous fans, but this one is out of control.

"Well, now that you mention it," Logan starts, giving me an apprehensive look before continuing. "As much as it pains me to say this as your agent, I think you should take some time off until this all blows over."

"You want me to take time off?" I ask, saying each word slowly as if they are foreign to me. Hell, they pretty much are.

It's been go, go, go ever since my first Academy Award. I never set out to be a movie star. I moved to L.A. right after college to pursue a business venture with a friend. That fell through and I was left broke and stuck in one of the most expensive cities in the country. Someone made an offhand comment about how I would make a good stuntman. What better place than Hollywood to try and find a gig?

Turns out I was pretty damn good at jumping through windows and surviving staged, yet still dangerous, car crashes and explosions. Oh, and falling. Lots and lots of falling. Down stairs, off buildings, even off an elephant during one of my early gigs.

A talent scout spotted me on set one day and introduced me to Logan, who encouraged me to step out from behind the scenes and audition for a leading role. My debut part – instead of being an actor's stunt double – was a box office hit. Eight years later and I'm still going strong.

"It's not just the stalker," Logan says. "We both know you've been in a bit of a...slump."

"Is this about me not taking that damn spy movie role?"

"It's about you not taking *any* roles for the last six months."

"That's not true. I was the host of *Saturday Night Live* last month," I protest. Logan gives me a look that says it all. It's a weak-ass argument and we both know it. "I'm also working on my screenplay," I mumble under my breath.

"You're too young to be transitioning into a writer/director career, Aiden. You're thirty, for chrissake."

"But—"

"This has been the plan from day one," he cuts me off. "I think you just need to step back and regroup. Find your passion again. Get inspired, you know? Then you'll start to see things more clearly. Besides, nothing will drive up ticket sales like Hollywood's golden boy going off the radar only to reappear better than ever in his next role."

"I don't know, Logan. I don't know anything anymore," I confess, looking at my vandalized car.

"Just think about it," he says, just as two cop cars pull into my driveway. I grunt at him, then wave at the officers, effectively ending the conversation.

***

It's four in the morning, and I haven't slept a wink. Logan's words from earlier ring true. I have been in a slump ever since my last movie wrapped up. If I'm being honest, I was in a slump long before taking my millionth role as an action hero.

I was in an indie film two years ago that totally tanked. It was my first dramatic role in a film I truly believed in, as opposed to the cookie-cutter action movies and occasional chick flicks I've built my career on.

As devastating as that whole ordeal was, it sparked the desire to write a meaningful screenplay and try my hand at directing. Of course, Logan was having none of that. He's kept me busy since then, always dodging me or shutting me down when I mention my screenplay.

Now that I think about it, a break might actually be good. Without my persistent agent breathing down my neck, maybe I can dedicate some serious time to writing.

The first rays of sunlight peek through my curtains, and despite my lack of sleep, I find myself smiling. Yes, a break is exactly what I need. Like Logan said, I need to be inspired, though not in the way he thinks. When I come back, it will be on my terms, as soon as I figure out what those are.

Where am I going, exactly, for this break? Definitely not any of the resorts and celebrity spas Logan emailed me information on as soon as he left my place last night. He even suggested I rent a private island. I have something much more low-key in mind. As soon as I get my best friend to agree, I'll be staying with him where we both grew up – Irving, Texas.

Not wanting to waste another second, I grab my phone and dial Josiah. I know he'll be awake even though it's barely six in the morning in Texas. The man is almost as much of a workaholic as I am, only he's focused his energy on being a doctor with his own private practice. He's my only connection to my old life, and we still make time to call each other every month or so.

"Damn, Aiden. I thought you entitled actors didn't start the day until noon," Josiah says by way of greeting.

"Shut up, asshole," I mutter before joining him in laughter.

"Are you just going to bed or waking up? I gotta know if I'm dealing with drunk Aiden or severely hungover Aiden."

"Neither. Plus, it's been a long time since I drunk dialed you."

"Ah, but what a call that was. I thought I knew everything about my best friend, but you somehow kept your love of Celine Dion from me until then."

"I only sang like two songs," I argue, though I'm on the verge of laughing.

"You sang five, including that depressing one from *Titanic*."

"Hey, *My Heart Will Go On* is a classic, and I won't apologize for trying to bring some culture into your life." I can't get through the sentence without chuckling, and Josiah joins me.

"Seriously, what's up?" he asks once the laughter has died down.

"My agent and I were talking about me taking a bit of a break, and I was hoping I could crash at your place for a few weeks."

"Everything okay?"

"Yeah, mostly." I fill him in on the stalker situation, at least what I know, which isn't much.

"Of course, you can stay with me, for however long you need. It'll be good to have you around. It's been too damn long since I've seen your ugly mug."

"Ugly? Pretty sure I won *People* magazine's "Sexiest Man Alive" last year."

"Ack, you know those things are more about money and politics than actual good looks." He's not wrong.

"Still better lookin' than you," I joke.

"Why am I agreeing to this again?"

"For the potential Celine Dion performances?"

This makes him chuckle. "Yeah, you're right. That's worth it. Oh, also, my sister is staying with me for the time being, but there's plenty of space for all of us. Sophia keeps mostly to herself these days; I doubt you'll even notice her."

"Thanks, man. I'm going to book a flight today if that's alright."

"Sure thing."

We hang up after the final arrangements are made. I send a text to Logan, knowing he won't read it until he wakes up in a few hours. By then, I hope to already be on a plane to Texas. I smile to myself, feeling pretty good about my plan. Yes, I can already tell everything will be different a few weeks from now.

Chapter 2

I load up my brush and drag it over the canvas, satisfied with the black streak it left behind. Like most of my obsessive paintings since the accident, it's dark and distorted. I can't help it. Art is a reflection of the soul, and right now, my soul is pretty fucking warped.

My parents were understanding at first, even uncharacteristically worried about me. I suppose your kid having a near-death experience will do that to even the most absent of parents. But their patience with me ran out when I opted out of my second year of college. I was already bitter about school in the first place, and after facing my own mortality, I needed to take some time to regroup and figure out what I really wanted out of life.

My parents pushed me to follow in their footsteps and get a law degree, but I knew I'd never make it as a lawyer. When they realized that was a losing battle, they suggested I become a doctor like my brother.

After about the tenth heated discussion about my future, my dad finally asked me what I wanted to study. When I confessed that I had already applied to a few art schools, my parents shared a laugh, then went right on talking about connections they have for great medical schools.

I expected them to be upset, not dismissive. But I didn't have much of a choice when they said they wouldn't pay for a useless degree. So, I let them steamroll right over me and my dreams, which lead me to enrolling at the local college for a nice, practical accounting degree.

Four months ago, however, everything changed. My parents had a few internships lined up for me over the summer, but Dad canceled them and said I should stay home and rest so I could focus on my schooling come fall.

Over the summer, I filled dozens of canvases with my twisted views of reality. Stroke after stroke, I wrote my pain into each piece. Stroke after stroke, I let the fear and uncertainty take control, my hands mere instruments at their mercy. Stroke after stroke, I began to heal. The darkness that settled over my heart was transferred onto the canvas, giving it a place to live and breathe without suffocating me.

I'm still a work in progress, like many of my paintings, but I feel like I finally have space in my head and heart to move forward, one step, one stroke at a time.

My first act of freedom was telling my parents about not going back to school in the fall, and possibly not at all. That was their breaking point. We got in a huge fight, but I didn't back down. Things ended when they told me I could either go back to school or find someplace else to live. I was shocked, though at that point I really shouldn't have been. Thankfully, my big brother stepped in and offered for me to stay in his pool house while I figured out my next move.

A loud bang followed by a crashing sound startles me from my thoughts. I jump at the disruptive noise and promptly spill paint all over my shirt. I can feel little drops on my cheek and forehead, which means I probably have paint in my hair, too. I love my brother, but he really needs to knock before barging in like this.

I turn around to give him an annoyed glare, but freeze when I see who is standing in the living room just a few feet away from me. It's not my brother. In fact, it's not anyone in my family. I haven't seen him face to face since he left for L.A. eight years ago, but all of the familiar emotions come flooding to the surface with just one look.

Aiden Steele.

Movie star. Heartthrob. Literally one of the most eligible, sexy bachelors on the market. But to me, he'll always be my first crush. I liked him before he went off and accidentally became famous. Ridiculous, I know. He probably doesn't even recognize me.

Aiden seems as startled by my presence as I am by his. We stare at each other in silence, me taking in his massive frame, sharp gray eyes, and the hint of stubble on his square jaw. God, he's even more impressive in person after all this time. Aiden was ridiculously attractive before he left, and of course, he's only become more swoon-worthy over the years. But knowing this and seeing him in person are two completely different things.

What the hell is he doing here? What is that look on his face? Are his gray eyes turning silver? Is that even possible? Has anyone ever melted into a puddle in his presence before? I feel like I'm about to do just that. Either melt or faint. Or possibly have a heart attack. My head, heart, and lady parts can't decide which one should take over, so I just stand here, staring at this god of a man while black paint drips down my forehead. Great first impression.

I watch with rapt attention as his full lips curve into a devastating grin. Good lord, how does anyone survive breathing the same air as Aiden Steele? I'm not fangirling, I swear. I was this bad around him before he moved away.

Aiden finally breaks the silence, as well as the spell he cast over me.

"I got you all dirty. Let me help clean you up."

Chapter 3

"I got you all dirty. Let me help clean you up." God, what a horrible line. I'm pretty sure I said that in a cheesy rom-com at one point in my career. Hell, after the first few films, they all blend together. All I know is that my game seriously sucks. I'm baffled by the perfectly disheveled beauty.

Her dark brown hair is piled on top of her head in a messy bun, allowing me to see the slope of her slender neck. I want to kiss it. Bite it. Lick it. I don't think I've ever found a neck sexy before, but Jesus, everything about this goddess draws me in. Her porcelain skin, thick curves, and slight blush have my dick roaring to life.

Even with black paint splattered over her cheek and forehead, she's undoubtedly the most exquisite woman I've ever seen. I want to taste her soft pink lips and kiss the freckles dotted over the bridge of her nose. Big, beautiful hazel eyes stare back at me, and it's then I realize I know who this ethereal creature is.

Sophia Turner, aka, Josiah's little sister.

Holy hell, when did she grow up? Fuck, I've been missing out. I suddenly want to know everything about her. What's her favorite book? Is she a coffee or tea person? Does she prefer hot weather to cool weather? What sounds does she make when she comes? Does she want children? Will she let me give them to her?

Calm the hell down, I chastise myself. I mean, seriously, what the hell?

"Um…I-I…excuse me," she stutters before turning on her heel and running away from me. I'm pretty sure that has never happened to me. I get the urge to chase her down, which is another new feeling.

I've been photographed with models and actresses while attending events, and I even had a "relationship" with one of my co-stars, but it was all a PR stunt. Yeah, that shit really happens. Josiah hit the nail on the head when he said it's all about politics and the bottom line.

As for a real, meaningful relationship? I haven't bothered. I learned early on the kind of people fame attracts. Shallow, manipulative, insincere people who *always* have an agenda. How could I possibly trust anyone enough to let them in?

One look at Sophia, however, and I'm starting to change my mind. Fuck it, I've already changed my mind. I get the feeling Sophia is going to change everything soon enough. I just hope I didn't already ruin my chances with my dumb suggestive comment.

I know I shouldn't be entertaining these thoughts for several reasons. First of all, she's ten years younger than me. Then there's the fact I'm only here for a few weeks before going back home, hundreds of miles away. Plus, I'm supposed to be working on my screenplay while I'm here, not obsessing over my best friend's little sister. And that's another thing. Probably the most important thing. She's Josiah's little sister.

I try to convince myself to walk away for all of two seconds before surrendering to whatever the hell is happening. I wanted passion, right? I wanted inspiration. I didn't expect it to come to me on my first day, let alone in the form of a curvy, tempting, and totally off-limits woman, but I can't deny the hold she already has over me.

The painting she was working on catches my eye. I take a few steps closer so I can study it better. I can make out the outline of a woman, but it's distorted. Blurred. Almost like I'm looking at the scene from underwater. The edges are composed of dark, angry brushstrokes that fade toward the center. Various shades of blue ripple across the canvas, obstructing large portions of the woman's face and figure.

I've been to my fair share of gallery openings and prestigious art exhibits, but never has a painting hit me square in the chest and sunk down into the depths of me. I feel the weight of her emotions the longer I examine the painting. Fear, uncertainty, anger, and a desperate, confusing longing crash into me like waves, one right after the other, until I'm drowning in her sorrow. Surrounded by it. Suffocating on it.

"It's not finished," comes a soft voice from behind me.

I turn around and look at Sophia. My lungs fill with air and the painting releases its hold on me when her hazel eyes meet mine. How did such a sweet little thing create the heartbreaking artwork behind me? What inspired such a beautifully devastating painting?

Sophia breaks eye contact, choosing to look at her feet instead. My gaze travels there as well, causing me to smile when I see her cute little bare feet. When she shuffles her weight from foot to foot, I realize she's uncomfortable. Embarrassed, even. Shit, I haven't said anything about what's clearly a very private and personal piece of art. I have to up my game if I want a chance with Sophia. Seducing this little goddess with a hidden pain is my new priority.

"This is incredible," I say, finally finding my words.

"Thanks, Aiden."

God, hearing my name on her lips sends a shiver down my spine and makes my already hard dick turn to granite. Swear to Christ I've never had such an instant, nearly crippling attraction to someone.

"I mean it, Sophia. Are you going to school for your art?"

She looks up at me and tilts her head to the side in an adorable, confused manner. "You know who I am?" She seems shocked. She's also avoiding my question.

"Of course. You know who I am, too," I smirk. She grins, and I know I'm well and truly fucked. I want to see it again. I want all of her smiles. I want to be the one to put them on her lovely face.

"I think that's a little bit different. It'd be more impressive if I somehow *didn't* know about Hollywood superstar Aiden Steele. Too bad I also know about how he once drank a fifth of tequila, ate seven hotdogs, and then promptly threw up all over his best friend's couch."

I throw my head back and laugh at the memory. "Yeah, that wasn't my most flattering moment," I agree. "In my defense, I was celebrating my twenty-first birthday."

"I bet it's a far cry from your last birthday party," she jokes.

"Actually, I was filming on location in Germany for my last birthday. I was too exhausted to do any celebrating. I went to my hotel and ordered room service, but I fell asleep before it was even delivered." I don't know why I told her all that, but I find I want to tell her everything about me.

Sophia studies me the same way I studied her painting. The way she's looking at me, picking me apart, trying to figure out who I am, makes me feel raw and exposed. It's terrifying and exhilarating and exactly what I've been missing. No one has taken the time to see me, understand me, or look past the movie star bullshit in far too long.

When she smiles at me, I swear my soul leaves my body and joins with hers. It knows where it belongs. Now I just have to get her to feel it, too. Once again, I remind myself to slow the hell down. I barely understand what's happening between us and I don't want to scare her off with my intensity.

I clear my throat and smile back at her. "So, uh, I take it your brother didn't tell you I'm going to be crashing here for a few weeks?"

Her eyes go wide and she shakes her head no. "Here in the pool house?"

"I'm not sure, exactly. I just got here from the airport and called Josiah, but he didn't answer. Then I wandered out here." Sophia nods, listening intently while I ramble. I can't seem to stop talking. "This is kind of a last minute trip for me. I called Josiah at six this morning and pretty much told him I'd be staying with him for a few weeks."

She tilts her head to the side again in the most adorable way. "I'm staying in the room out here for now, but I can show you one of the guest rooms in the main house if you want," she offers.

I do want. I want very much. But if I get her within five feet of a bed, I might toss her down on it and sink into her sweet little pussy. Though my dick likes the thought of that, I still have a few brain cells left to remind me I'm moving way too damn fast.

"I can figure it out," I say, clearing my throat. "I'm probably just going to crash anyway. I don't want to distract you from your painting. I can't wait to see the finished piece."

She blushes again, those cute round cheeks of hers just begging me to kiss them.

"The code to get in is forty-seven twenty-eight."

"Thanks, love." I smile and wink at her before heading toward the door. I don't know why I called her that, but I don't regret it. In fact, I think I'll be calling her that from now on.

Chapter 4

Sophia

"What now?" I mutter to myself when my phone dings, notifying me of a new email.

It's too dang early to be inundated with internship opportunities from my mother, but I know if I don't respond, she'll just keep at it. Even though we haven't talked face to face in over a month, she still finds a way to assert her wishes on my life. Her last email explains that I shouldn't be wasting my time during my "temporary hiatus from school".

I snort-laugh when I see her closing line. *I've attached a recipe for a kale and chia breakfast smoothie. Just because you're on a break doesn't mean you should be eating carbs and sugar for breakfast.*

A smirk spreads across my lips when I look at the half-eaten croissant slathered in jam and butter in my hand. *Fuck you*, I think to myself as I finish it off in three large, satisfying bites.

"What'd that pastry ever do to you?"

I stop mid-chew and look up from my phone. Aiden is leaning against the kitchen counter, grinning at me. Oh crap, I didn't make him up. He really barged in on me when I was painting yesterday. My cheeks heat just thinking about him looking at my dark thoughts as they dripped from the canvas. He saw me, saw my heart, and he called it incredible.

I look up into his captivating eyes. Today they are more blue than gray. He raises an eyebrow, smirking at me while waiting for my answer. What did he ask me, again? Oh, right. He saw me take my anger out on an unsuspecting croissant. Damn, I need to get it together.

I shrug and stand up from the table, needing to go back to the pool house and cool down. "Sometimes a girl just has to smash some carbs early in the morning, you know?"

His eyes light up, making my heart do silly things, like hope for a future with my first and only crush. "Noted," he says, his smooth voice pouring over me. Is everything about this man designed to make my panties wet?

Looking away from the unattainable Aiden, I slip past him to put my dishes in the sink. He surprises me by looping his fingers around my wrist and pulling me close. His eyes roam over my face, making me aware of the fact that I literally rolled out of bed less than thirty minutes ago. I didn't even brush my hair, let alone wash my face or put on makeup.

Aiden doesn't seem to mind. In fact, if I didn't know better, I'd say he likes what he sees. He dips his head down so our faces are only a few inches apart. One of his hands comes up to cup the side of my face. Aiden's touch is so gentle, which is surprising coming from such a large, chiseled mountain of a man. I'm hardly aware of what I'm doing, but my body acts all on its own. My head tilts up and my lips part, waiting for his kiss.

Instead, Aiden wipes his thumb over the corner of my mouth, collecting a drop of jam.

Oh my God. How embarrassing! I'm about to die of shame when Aiden licks the jam off his thumb and gives me a smoldering gaze. Holy hell, I think I'm going to burst into flames. Is he being flirty? Does he find me as attractive as I find him? No. No way. He's a freaking actor. Of course, he knows how to make women swoon.

I spin out of his arms, but he grabs my hand. I toss him what I hope is a playful look, though I'm not sure I pulled it off. "Your movie star charm isn't going to work on me," I say with more confidence than I feel.

His eyes turn dark silver like they did yesterday, and good lord, I really need to get away from him before I make an even bigger fool of myself.

"I guess I'll have to try harder then," he murmurs before lifting my hand up to his lips. Aiden never breaks eye contact as he presses a tender kiss on the inside of my wrist.

I try to hold back the shiver that travels up my arm and through my body, but I know Aiden sees it when he gives me another one of those sexy smirks. He drops my hand and winks at me before walking out of the kitchen. I'm left gaping after him, my skin still tingling where his lips made contact.

How long is he staying here, again? And how am I supposed to resist the totally out of my league, off-limits, ridiculously attractive, and surprisingly sweet movie star?

Chapter 5

Aiden

"Ah, fuckin' goddamnit! *Ow!*"

I lose my balance and topple to the floor, admitting defeat. I press pause on the "Easy Yoga for Beginners" video I found on YouTube and then assume my position lying flat on the floor, cursing the mislabeled video.

I'm supposed to be relaxing, but I don't know how. I've heard yoga is great for your mind and body, so I thought, what the hell? Might as well give it a shot now that I have some downtime. Yeah...not so much. How the fuck do people stretch like that? I discovered new ways to hurt my muscles, which is actually kind of impressive.

I sigh and scrub a hand down my face. Maybe I'm having trouble relaxing because I'm still all keyed up from my encounter with Sophia this morning. I walked into the kitchen and saw her sitting at the table, scrolling through her phone. She hadn't seen me yet, so I took the opportunity to study her.

She rolled her eyes at something she was reading on her phone, then gave the croissant in her hand a defiant, determined glare before finishing it off. For some reason, the whole scene made me want to sweep her up in my arms and kiss her cute little nose. At the same time, I had the urge to bend her over the table and slam my cock into her over and over until we both came apart, screaming each other's name.

Shaking my head of those thoughts, I look over at the clock in my temporary room and see it's almost eleven. Damn. I thought for sure it'd be two or three in the afternoon. Maybe a vacation wasn't the best idea.

After a quick shower, I get my laptop out and open up my screenplay. If I can't relax and do nothing, I might as well be productive. Usually it takes me a while to get into the groove of writing, but today I can hardly type fast enough to keep up with the words and ideas in my head.

I'm startled out of the writing bubble I was in by the sound of someone rummaging around in the kitchen. I look at the time on my computer and see it's six in the evening. Holy shit. Scrolling through the document, I'm shocked to see I wrote over thirty-five pages.

I save my progress and stand up, stretching out my aching muscles. Yeah, doing yoga and then sitting for seven hours was a bad idea. I might have to try out the pool later tonight and see if a soak and a swim will help. The fact that the pool is right outside the place where Sophia is staying is just an added bonus.

When I get to the kitchen, I find my curvy queen stirring something on the stove, shaking her hips to some song playing on her phone. For the second time today, I quietly observe her and take in her beauty.

She turns her head to look at me over her shoulder. Damn, those hazel eyes shine with excitement, and a wide, genuine smile spreads across her face. When's the last time someone was just plain happy to see me?

"Hey," she says, breaking me out of my thoughts. "Josiah has a few late appointments tonight, so he won't be home for a bit. I figured you might be a little lost in the kitchen without a personal chef."

"I can cook!" I insist. "I just haven't done it a while," I say with a grin. She grins right back. Every smile I get out of her feels like a victory. I don't know what Sophia has been through, but I know any twenty-year-old who is living with their sibling and producing heartbreaking paintings like the one I saw has a story to tell.

"Uh-huh," she says skeptically, raising an eyebrow at me. "Tonight, you'll have to make do with a California scramble and a side of hash browns."

"California, huh?"

She shrugs as she dishes up dinner and walks over to the table with our plates. The sway in her hips has my hands twitching to grab her and pull her down into my lap.

"Seemed appropriate. Just in case you're missing home."

"I'm right where I belong," I say, looking up at her from my seat as she sets my plate down on the table.

Sophia gives me a meaningful look and then nods slowly. "Yeah. For the first time in a long time, I feel like I'm right where I belong, too."

Chapter 6

Sophia

I can't believe I admitted that to him, but his honesty encouraged me to be honest as well. This moment feels significant. Intense. A little too real, especially considering the dirty thoughts I had about him last night. Oh, and not to mention the fact that his status as an unattainable movie star and my brother's best friend hasn't changed.

I step away, breaking whatever connection we just shared. Putting some much needed distance between us, I sit down across from Aiden instead of next to him. I'm not sure what to say, but thankfully he takes the lead.

"Have you ever done yoga?"

I jerk my head up from where I was staring down at my food. "What?" I ask, laughing a bit at his random question.

"Yoga. I tried it today and it nearly destroyed me."

I stare at him for a second before I release the laughter building inside of me. Picturing the muscled action hero sitting across from me doing a cat-cow pose is just too funny. I cover my mouth with my hand, trying to contain my giggle, but it's too late.

Aiden narrows his eyes at me, and I think for a moment I've offended him. He joins me a second later, the deep, rich sound of his laughter warming me up and filling me with more joy than I've felt in a long time.

"Yeah, it's not for the faint of heart," I agree.

He nods and sighs dramatically. "You're telling me."

We share a smile before digging into our food. A comfortable silence falls over us while we eat. Everything about Aiden makes me feel comfortable, which is something I haven't felt even before the accident.

I don't know why he has this calming effect on me or why I feel like I could tell him anything. Then it hits me. I can be myself around him. I don't have to pretend to fit into a certain mold like my parents want. I don't have to plaster on a smile on the rare occasion I meet up with a friend for lunch and they ask how I'm doing. For the first time in so damn long I feel like...like I can breathe.

"You know what adventures I had today, so tell me what you were up to," Aiden says before shoveling more food into his mouth. "Besides cooking an amazing dinner, that is." It makes me unreasonably happy to know he likes my cooking.

"Mostly just painting," I shrug, picking at my food. It sounds lame when I say it out loud. All my days are pretty much the same. I'm no closer to figuring out what I want to do with my life now than when I first moved in.

"Good," Aiden says, surprising me. When I give him a questioning look, he smiles softly, making my insides melt. "You're creating something really meaningful. I may have only seen one unfinished painting, but that was enough to know you're brilliant and brave."

"Brave?"

"Yeah. It takes guts to face the kind of pain you released onto the canvas. Even if no one else sees it, that painting is a reminder of what you've fought through. I think that's really inspiring, Sophia."

I want to hide from him and his words, but I can't seem to look away from his gray eyes. Aiden means every single word he said, which makes me believe it, too. "Th-thanks," I stutter out, unsure of how else to respond. "So, um...what are you up to the rest of the night?" I ask, wanting to change the subject.

"I was thinking I'd hit the pool after dinner settles. You should join me."

My heart stops and then slams against my chest as my stomach rolls violently. The thought of being in the water again makes me break out in a cold, clammy sweat.

"*No,*" I nearly shout, my voice harsher than I meant it to be. I close my eyes and take a deep breath, swallowing the panic back down. "I-I mean, no thanks. I, uh, I'll probably just go to bed early." I cringe at my reaction and at my stupid attempt at recovery.

Aiden furrows his brow and looks like he's about to say something, but then decides against it. Good. If he pried any further, I might just break down and ugly cry, which is the absolute last thing I want to do in front of him.

He clears his throat, and smiles at me, changing his demeanor from concerned to relaxed. It makes me relax, too. "Are you taking any classes this semester?"

Well, dang. That peace didn't last long. I guess we're hitting up all of my sore spots today.

"No..." I trail off, trying to figure out how much I want to tell him. "I'm taking some time off. I realized over the summer that I...uh, I just needed a break. Figure out what I really want out of life instead of following the path my parents planned out for me." It's not a lie, it's just not the whole truth. He doesn't know the catalyst for my change of heart.

"I think that's great," he says with zero judgment in his voice. "I'm doing the same thing. I understand the feeling of having your life dictated by something or someone else. I needed to take a break, too. Get inspired, you know?"

"Is it working?"

Aiden's sears me with a look, his eyes turning into liquid silver once again. I'm hit with a sudden overwhelming need to be closer to him. I want to feel his touch. His kiss. I want to feel him everywhere. My skin is on fire as a shiver spreads throughout my body.

And then his lips curl into a seductive smile, one that promises pleasure and sweet torture in equal measure. Good lord, it's intimidating how sexy this man is.

"I'm certainly inspired to do *something*," he purrs, his voice low and smooth as it washes over me cand makes my clit throb. I squirm in my seat, pressing my thighs together to try and find some relief from the constant ache I seem to have every time he looks at me.

I clear my throat and look away from him, reminding myself he's an actor. He's probably used that panty-melting grin on countless women.

That thought has me standing up and clearing off the plates. I need to get out of the line of fire. If he keeps shooting me those looks, I might forget that kissing him would be a bad idea.

Or the best idea, my apparently horny inner monologue suggests.

I reach out for Aiden's empty plate, but he grabs my wrist in a firm but gentle hold. He takes my plate out of my other hand as he scoots his chair back. Aiden tugs me closer to him, settling me in between his spread legs. I'm helpless to do anything but follow his lead.

He looks up at me, letting me see his desire. His hunger. His need. God, I really shouldn't, but I need him, too. I feel his large hands skim up the back of my bare thighs until he reaches the hem of my shorts. Slipping just his thumbs underneath the fabric, he caresses my skin, making my legs tremble and my breath catch in my throat.

Aiden takes advantage of my nearly debilitating arousal and pulls me closer, his hands wrapping around my thighs and urging me to straddle him. I hesitate slightly, but I can't look away from his intense gaze. It's more than lust shining in his eyes, there's tenderness as well. I don't know how that's even possible, but it's true.

I surrender to him completely, letting him settle me on his lap. He grunts in approval, the sound traveling through me and making my pussy clench.

"I knew you'd feel amazing," he says softly, more to himself than to me.

Aiden grips my hips and helps me rock against his hardening length. My hands glide up his chest and shoulders, then I tangle my fingers in his hair, pulling his head back so he has to look at me. I don't know what I'm doing, I just know I need more. Every part of me responds to every part of him. When his breaths grow shallow, mine do, too. When he rolls his hips, I do, too. When he groans and closes his eyes, I do, too.

When I open them again, I see Aiden looking right at me. His jaw clenches and his nostrils flare. I feel his hands slide from my hips down to my ass. He cups me there, squeezing the soft flesh and grinding my body down on his.

"Aiden..." I gasp, tightening my grip on his hair, pulling on the strands as a surge of pleasure rolls through me, making my muscles tense and my thighs shake.

"Sophia," he growls right before pressing his lips to mine.

His kiss destroys me. It's slow, soft, and seductive, shredding me into little ribbons of pliant pleasure. He sinks into me like I'm some decadent dessert, loving my mouth while his hands grip me tightly and crush me into his hard body.

I whimper into his mouth, making him groan. Aiden slips his hands under my shirt, letting them wander up and down the bare skin of my back. God, I can't seem to control my body from rubbing against his, my pussy grinding down on him, my nipples scraping against the hard planes of his chest.

"More," I whisper into his slightly parted lips before pulling the bottom one through my teeth. "I need more, Aiden."

Chapter 7

Aiden

"Fuck," I growl before claiming her lips once more. Sophia's hips touch up and down in my lap as she whimpers into my mouth. I deepen the kiss, licking up all of her sweetness.

Sliding one hand down her back, I dip my fingers into her shorts and grip her ass. Sophia gasps and whimpers as I squeeze her soft flesh. My other hand finds the button of her jean shorts and pops it open.

"Yes," Sophia whispers, her hot breath tickling my ear.

I stroke her over her underwear, growling when I feel how fucking *drenched* she is. "You need this, baby? Need me to make this pussy come?"

Sophia buries her face into the side of my neck, moaning loudly as I rub her clit through the soaked fabric of her cotton panties. Her hips jerk as she grinds down on my hand. I don't think she's even aware she's doing it, but her body certainly knows what it needs.

"So bad. I need it so bad, Aiden." Fuck, her voice is a half desperate whisper and half sexy moan. The combination has me thrusting my own hips and squeezing her ass harder, helping her roll her soft curves against me.

After teasing her a bit more, I slip my hand inside her panties and glide my fingers through her wet folds, scooping up her juices and circling her clit.

"Aiden!" Sophia gasps, sounding almost shocked.

"You okay?" I grunt, sounding more animal than human. I'm all fucking animal right now. I've never felt such a primal need to claim someone and mark them as mine. God, I want to bite her. Fuck her. Love her forever.

"S-so g-good," she moans, resting her forehead on mine and squeezing her eyes shut.

"So tight," I murmur to myself as my finger circles her pulsing entrance. Sophia whimpers and angles her hips, positioning herself right over the tip of my finger. I groan and push my thick digit inside of her, just a little bit.

Slowly, I work my finger in and out of her swollen entrance while grinding the heel of my palm down on her clit. Sophia trembles in my arms and her nails dig into my shoulders as she clings to me. She's *right* there, I can tell. So close to her sweet release. I feel her body tightening, her muscles tensing, her pussy clenching around me, bracing for her orgasm.

"Aiden...oh God, I..."

She holds her breath, her entire body teetering on the edge, waiting for me to push her off into pure, sweet ecstasy.

And then the front door swings open.

Sophia sears me with the most excruciating look. Her eyes are wide with shock and a little fear, but more than that, they are shimmering with frustrated, almost painful tears, knowing she won't get the release I've been teasing out of her.

As much as it fucking kills me, I help her off my lap and steady her when her knees shake. She hasn't said anything yet, her eyes still foggy with lust and pent-up need. I bend down and kiss her temple before whispering, "Wait for me in the pool house. I promise I'll finish what I started."

With that, I gently turn her around so she's facing the sliding glass door leading out to the pool house. I give her juicy ass a little spank to send her off. This seems to wake Sophia up a bit. She looks at me over her shoulder, her lips swollen from my kisses, her cheeks flushed from her almost-orgasm. I bite back a groan when she smiles at me. Fuck, I want to follow her right now, shove her against the wall, fuck her so damn hard...

"Hey guys!" Josiah calls from where he is in the living room. Thank God the kitchen and dining room are a distance from the front door.

"Just me," I say, adjusting my aching dick before he comes in and sees the condition I'm in.

"I figured," Josiah responds, his voice much closer now that he's in the same room. I managed to walk the three feet to the sink so I could rinse off our dishes and have an excuse to hide my massive erection from the last person on the planet I want to know about it. "Glad you figured out dinner on your own, sorry I've had to work late your first two nights here."

"No need to apologize. I'm the one who invited myself for a visit. How's work going, anyway?"

Josiah tells me about some of his patients and fills me in on everything that's changed around town since the last time I was here. We share a beer and shoot the shit for about an hour before Josiah yawns and calls it a night.

I watch him go up the stairs, and then I deflate on the couch, letting out a huge breath. I've missed hanging out with my best friend. I know I should feel guilty for lusting after his sister, but it's not just lust. I feel like I already need her in a desperate, overwhelming way. I tasted her need for me, too. Not just a physical need, either. I don't know what she needs exactly, but I need it, too. I need to be that for her, and I intend to start tonight.

When I hear Josiah's door close, I wait a few minutes, then slip out the side door and head straight for the pool house.

Taking a deep breath, I raise my hand to knock on the sliding door of the pool house, but it opens before I get the chance. Sophia stands in the doorway, looking up at me with questions in her big, hazel eyes. I take a step closer, placing a hand on her hip to guide her backward until we're both inside.

Her eyes never leave mine as I press her against the wall. I take a moment to appreciate the beauty in front of me. Moonlight spills over the left side of her face and down her ample cleavage. I take in her curves, her creamy skin, the way her chest is rising and falling with shallow breaths.

Cupping the back of her neck, I pull Sophia closer to me, brushing my lips against hers. Her breath rolls over my skin, the sensation echoing throughout my body and making my cock twitch. I want to tear her little robe off and fuck her against this wall. I want to rip her apart and ruin her for all other men. I want to make her sob with pleasure and scream my name until her voice gives out.

Instead, I sip at her lips, coaxing her tongue to tangle with mine. Her hands slide up my chest and she grabs my shirt, pulling me closer. I deepen our kiss, running my hands up her thighs and under the hem of her short, silky robe.

When I feel her bare ass, I tear my mouth away from hers and growl savagely. Sophia rests her head against the wall and closes her eyes. I dip my head down and kiss her neck, nipping and licking at the sensitive spot below her ear.

"I thought you changed your mind," she whispers.

"Never," I grunt, continuing to explore her soft, sweet body with my hands and mouth. I place kisses down her neck and across her collarbone, grasping the material of her robe with my teeth and pulling it aside.

The white silk falls to the side, and I stare in awe at her big, round breast as it's revealed to me. I have my mouth on her in the next second, sucking on her nipple while sliding a hand between her thighs. I cup her pussy, groaning when I feel her wet heat.

"I need you," she whimpers. "I need you, Aiden."

"I've got you, love. I'll give you everything." I scoop her up in my arms and carry her over to her bed, laying her down gently. I stare down at my girl, her brown hair fanning out around her face, her white silk rope hanging open, the silver moonlight bathing her body, highlighting her ample curves. "Sophia..." I whisper, not quite believing she's actually here, offering herself to me.

She tries to cover herself up, mistaking my awed silence for disapproval. I remove her hands from her stomach and set them back down at her sides before climbing on top of her, holding myself up on my forearms on either side of her head. She parts her legs for me, allowing me to settle in between them.

"Um...shouldn't you take some clothes off, too?" Sophia grins, trying to be flirty, but I see the nervousness and hesitation in her eyes.

I smile back at her and kiss her cheek and temple before nuzzling into the side of her neck. "Not tonight, love. Tonight is about you."

"What do you mean?"

I lift my head up and smirk at her, loving the adorably confused look on her face. "Let me show you."

Before she can say anything else, I kiss the breath out of her lungs, only stopping when she pulls away to gasp for air. I kiss and nibble down her neck, between her breasts, lower, lower, lower, leaving kisses over every inch of her body.

By the time I get to her juicy little cunt, Sophia is writhing beneath me, her eyes closed, her head tilted back, her fists clenched around the sheets. I pry her legs open, guiding one over my shoulder and then the other.

"Jesus Christ," I grunt, staring at her dripping pink folds. Her hard little clit is pulsing, begging for attention.

"Aiden," she moans, bowing her back off the mattress in an attempt to get me closer.

God, she's still strung so tight from not coming earlier in the kitchen. I feel the frustration, adrenaline, and tension vibrate throughout her body. "Gonna take care of this pussy, Sophia. Gonna make you feel so good," I promise before taking my first taste.

I flatten my tongue and lick her from bottom to top, slowly, savoring every inch of her. I swirl the tip of my tongue over her clit, then suck it into my mouth. Sophia lets go of the sheets, choosing to claw at my back instead. I fucking love it.

"What are you doing to me?" she gasps before letting out a loud, wanton moan. I rock my hips against the mattress, needing some sort of relief for myself. Fuck, she's not the only one who's aching right now.

I answer her question by thrusting my tongue into her pulsing channel, lapping up her sweet cream straight from the source. She twists beneath me, but I lay my forearm across her hips, pinning her down while I devour her little cunt.

I bring her right to the edge and keep her there. Her muscles draw up tight, her joints lock, and she sucks in a breath of air, her entire body frozen in place.

I scrape my teeth across her clit, and she comes like a fucking goddess on my tongue. Her juices coat my face as I suck and lick and fucking destroy her pussy. She's shaking so hard I have to grip her hips to keep her in place. But I don't stop. Not for a second.

Sophia convulses beneath me as I growl into her cunt, pushing her deeper into her orgasm, making her feel all of it. A strangled cry leaves her lips as she comes again. I cover her mouth, muffling her screams as I drink down her release.

Her fingers tangle in my hair and she holds me as she fucks my face. Sophia circles her hips, completely lost in her lust and pleasure. I'm lost in her. Completely consumed by her scent, her taste, her softness, and how she feels in my hands.

I lick her to a final, fierce, and trembling orgasm. She snaps her legs around my head as she reaches her peak, then Sophia goes completely limp, melting into the mattress. I jump off the bed and whip out my cock, stroking the fucker hard and fast.

"Sophia," I snarl, once again more animal than human.

"Aiden," she whimpers, following the motion of my hand.

I lose my shit when she licks her lips. I grip my angry fucking cock and jerk myself off almost violently. Sophia senses my need and spreads her legs for me, then cups her breasts, pushing them together.

Goddamn, how did I get so lucky?

I let go of every-fucking-thing and come on her tits and pussy. Rope after rope of my sticky release coats her skin, and damn, it has to be the sexiest thing I've ever seen. My body moves on its own, my hands gliding over her heated skin, rubbing my cum into her, marking her like a beast.

Sophia takes a shuddering breath and then grabs my hands, tugging me down on top of her. I take her lips in a wild, desperate kiss, then break it off to gasp for air. Rolling over on my back, I take my woman with me, draping her sweaty, cum-covered body over my chest. This is the most content and satisfied I've ever been, and I've only really known Sophia for a day.

"You okay?" I ask once we've both caught our breath.

"So good," she sighs, snuggling into my side.

I kiss the top of her head and run my fingers up and down her spine. "Good," I whisper into her hair. "Get some rest, baby."

Sophia mumbles something, already half asleep. I chuckle and hold her close, soaking up every minute I can with her before I have to go back to my room.

Chapter 8

Sophia

I set up my easel an hour ago, but I've yet to put a single stroke of paint on the canvas. Instead, I've been watching Aiden swim laps in the pool.

Watching the water slide over his back and arms as he swims away from me has me itching to go out there to get a better look. If I weren't such a coward, I'd throw on a swimsuit and join him, but that's out of the question for so many reasons.

Aiden does that underwater flip thing when he gets to the other side of the pool, pushing off the wall and launching himself back in my direction. When he breaks through the water, I literally find myself drooling.

He's been staying here for a few days now, and we haven't done anything like our encounter his second night here. My face heats, as well as other, lower parts of me, when I think about it. The way Aiden took control, covered me in kisses, made me come over and over until I couldn't move.

As incredible as that was, the thing I've replayed in my head every night since is the way he tore at his jeans to get his cock out. The way he stroked himself with a wild, desperate need. The dark look in his eyes as he stared at every inch of my body made me spread my legs and grip my breasts like a porn star. Only he could bring that out in me.

Since that night, Aiden and I have shared a few heated moments and stolen glances, but mostly we've talked. I've told him things I barely even knew about myself, and he's confided in me as well. I knew life as a movie star isn't everything it's cracked up to be, but I had no idea how lonely Aiden was. I don't think he realized it either until he arrived here.

He also told me about having a stalker, though he didn't divulge much more information than that. I can respect his privacy. Lord knows I have secrets of my own.

Josiah has made a point to come home earlier in the evenings so we can all have dinner together. It's nice hanging out and socializing more than I have in months, but it also makes me feel guilty as hell for wanting Aiden the way I do.

I focus my attention back on the object of my childhood, and now adulthood, obsession. Today his eyes are clear blue like the water, but when he locks his gaze on mine, they turn gray. I can't help the wet ache that forms between my thighs.

He smirks at me like he knows I've been eyeing him up like a piece of meat for the better part of an hour. I haven't exactly been subtle, and the bay window I'm standing in front of does nothing to hide my thirsty glances.

When Aiden reaches the end of the pool closest to my window, he pulls himself halfway up, resting his arms over the side of the pool. He winks at me and then tips his head to the side in a silent invitation to swim with him.

I immediately shake my head no and try looking away from him, but I can't. His gaze won't release mine. Aiden smiles that stupid, crazy hot smile of his and nods slowly, trying to charm me into the pool.

I want to. I really, *really* do. I don't mind being near water or looking at it, so staying in the pool house hasn't been an issue at all. But actually *going in* the water? Not so much. Not since that day. My parents, friends, and pretty much everyone except Josiah has told me I need to get back out there, but how?

I'm broken. It broke me. I still have nightmares where I wake up gasping for air and clawing at my throat. My chest tightens at the thought of dipping even one toe into the water. I barely have the darkness under control as it is. It only goes away when I pick up a paintbrush and get it all out on the canvas. But what if that's not enough? Will I ever be normal?

Aiden watches me battle through my thoughts, never taking his eyes off mine. It's unnerving, to be so thoroughly studied by him while having all these raw, vulnerable thoughts. But something about being seen like this makes me feel brave. He's not backing down. My baggage doesn't scare him. The complications of us being together don't scare him. Nothing, it seems, scares Aiden Steele.

His bravery makes me want to be brave.

I drink in all the strength and encouragement he's giving me from just one look through the window. Then I nod my head slightly and run to my room to change into my swimsuit before I chicken out.

With shaky hands, I dig through the closet and find an old swimsuit from when I was in high school. It's not anything special, just a black two-piece tankini, but that doesn't matter. I throw it on as quickly as possible, my courage draining with each second I'm away from Aiden. Grabbing a towel from the linen closet, I take a deep breath and head out toward the pool.

Aiden has the biggest smile on his face. I've only ever seen him smile like this when he's accepting awards, though not all of them. Certainly his first Academy Award. God, I remember watching him walk up on that stage and grin with pure joy, pride, and satisfaction. Why is he giving me the same look?

I shuffle my way toward the shallow end of the pool, where the stairs are. The confidence and bravery of just a few minutes ago fade with each step, but I drag one foot in front of the other until I'm standing a few inches from the top stair.

Aiden says something, but I can't hear him over the blood rushing in my ears. The shallow end is three feet deep. I *know* this. I *know* nothing bad is going to happen. But tell that to my clogged throat and burning lungs. I feel like I'm drowning, and I haven't even stepped foot into the damn pool.

"I'm right here, Sophia. Take it slow." Aiden's soft, calming voice pierces through my panic, just enough to allow me to focus on him instead of the water.

I didn't realize he was standing on the third stair down, making us almost eye level. He meets my gaze with a warm, patient smile. He's not judging me at all, even though I'm sure my behavior is odd. Aiden holds his hand out to help me into the pool. Why do I feel like he's offering so much more?

I look between his outstretched hand and his silver-blue eyes, both promising strength and safety. Lifting a trembling hand, I place it in his, knowing full well I'm giving him my heart as well.

He pulls me forward slightly, and my instinct is to jerk back. He keeps a firm hold on my hand, however, not letting me give in to the fear.

"I've got you," he murmurs. "Do you trust me, Sophia?" I nod and look up into his eyes once more, letting him see that I trust him with everything. "The first step is the hardest, but I promise I'm right here. I won't let anything happen to you."

Aiden pulls me forward once again, but this time, I let him. I grip the railing with one hand and squeeze his fingers with the other. My eyes never leave his as my right foot sinks down onto the first step, now fully submerged in water. I gasp a little at the shock, but I'm not frozen with fear. Aiden's eyes flash with pride and patience like he knows what a big deal this is, even though we still have a long way to go.

"That's it, love," he whispers his encouragement. His endearment for me momentarily makes me forget everything. Whenever that word falls from his lips, I want to throw myself into his arms and kiss him.

I'm jerked back into the moment when I feel the cool water hit my stomach. My throat closes up and I claw at the railing, needing it to pull myself to safety. I try telling Aiden to let me go, but all that comes out is some strangled whimper.

He pries my hand away from the railing, momentarily spiking my panic until he rests both of my hands on his shoulders. Aiden grips my hips and holds me close while I burrow into him.

"I've got you. I'm right here," he murmurs. I nod into his chest and let him soothe me. I can feel the water move around us, indicating he's pulling me in deeper, but I'm not afraid. After a few moments of wading in the pool, Aiden kisses my temple and grazes his lips against the shell of my ear. "Wrap your legs around my waist," he whispers. I do as he says, trusting this man with all of me. My life, my heart, my fears, my darkness.

I cling to him as he slowly walks around the pool with me in his arms. I know I should feel ridiculous, and a part of me does, especially since he has no idea why I'm behaving like this. But Aiden doesn't make me feel ashamed or embarrassed or anything other than safe and seen.

Maybe that's why I find myself confessing everything to him.

"I almost drowned four months ago," I whisper from where my face is buried into the side of his neck. Aiden stops moving, stops breathing, and I swear his heart stops beating for a second. Then he tightens his hold on me and resumes walking, giving me space to say whatever I need to say while slowly getting used to being in the water again. "I was out on a boat with some friends from school. We were tubing and..." I close my eyes against the memory, feeling the world grow smaller and press against my lungs.

"I've got you, Sophia. You're safe. I'm ready to listen whenever you're ready to talk." He adjusts his hold on me so he can rub calming circles on my back. His tender touch helps me breathe a little easier, but mostly it's his steady presence and unshakable strength that give me the courage to tell him the rest.

"We were about to head to shore for the day, but a few other girls convinced me I couldn't have a day on the lake without tubing at least once. They were juniors and I was just a freshman, and I so desperately wanted their approval. It's stupid, I know." I shrug. "The driver gunned the boat and did a tight circle so the inner tube bounced on the waves. I still don't know what happened exactly. When the tube flipped, I freaked out and grabbed the rope tying it to the boat instead of just crashing into the water and waiting for them to swing around to pick me up, like I should have done. I got a hold of the rope, but..."

A sob escapes my lips, but Aiden just holds me and soothes me, and whispers how safe I am and how he'll never let anything happen to me. He doesn't pressure me for more, but now that I've started, I need to get it all out there. It's the first time I've talked about it since my parents picked me up from the hospital.

"The rope got tangled and wrapped around my neck," I continue, my voice still unsteady. "It was…" I try finding the words, but once again, my mind is filled with darkness. I see brutal waves crashing and breaking above me, while darkness claws at me from below. I get brief glimpses of the bright Texas sky, but it's distorted, blurry, detached. Much like everything else since that day. I feel the rope tighten around my neck and drag me along.

"Breathe for me, Sophia," Aiden says, bringing me back from the edge of panic. "Just breathe for me, baby. It's all over now."

I nod my head and cry into his chest, feeling the truth of his words sink into me. *It's over. It's over.* The words unlock something deep inside, some hidden darkness I could never bring out in my art. He holds me while it works its way out of the recesses of my soul, hurting, healing, and finally leaving me empty in his arms.

Chapter 9

Aiden

I almost lost her before I even had her. That realization slams into my chest and makes me break out in a cold sweat, but I swallow down my own fear and focus on hers. I can't explain it, but I feel it leaving her trembling body with each ragged breath. I don't know what to do or say, so I just hold my Sophia close and cover her with my love and protection.

Her confession makes me want to jump out of the pool and wrap her up in a towel and tell her she never has to even look at water again if she doesn't want to. But that's not how healing works. Pain only goes away once it's been seen, felt, and appreciated for the lesson it taught you.

Sophia finally lifts her head up from where she was crying into my shoulder, letting me see her anguish mixed with hope. Tears wet her cheeks, but a tentative smile curls up one side of her lips. Her eyes, though swollen and lined in red from crying, are breathtaking. The swirls of greens, blues, and browns in her irises shine with a few flecks of gold that weren't there before. It's her light. It's shining through. Fuck if I don't have tears in my own eyes, thinking maybe I had something to do with giving that back to her.

"You're so strong, Sophia," I murmur, brushing her tears away with my thumb. I still have my other arm tucked under her thighs, holder her up and keeping her close to me. "I can't even imagine..." I close my eyes and rest my forehead on hers. There's so much I want to say, but don't know how. I realize she must have felt the same way. "That's what your painting is about," I say more to myself than to her.

"Yeah," she whispers. "I have dozens of them. Different scenes, but all dark and distorted. The feeling of being suffocated never left me, but now it sneaks up when I'm in crowds or when it's too noisy, or sometimes for no reason at all. I couldn't explain it to my parents when they demanded to know why I didn't sign up for classes in the fall. I couldn't explain it to my friends who were on the boat, or even those who weren't. They got tired of me having panic attacks, and eventually just..." Sophia shrugs, looking lost and hurt, but so fucking pure and strong, though she doesn't know it yet.

"So, you expressed yourself through your art," I prompt, not wanting her to focus on her shitty parents and friends who couldn't be bothered.

Sophia nods and gives me another tentative smile. I'll treasure every one of them. "I've always loved to paint. I wanted to go to art school, but I already told you how well that worked out." I grunt, remembering when she told me her parents' reaction. "After everything happened, I became obsessed with painting. It wasn't a desire, but a need. I *had* to get my fucked-up thoughts out, I had to see them, feel them, hate them, and eventually accept them."

"And have you? Accepted them?" I ask softly.

"I..." She looks at me thoughtfully, her hazel eyes brighter than I've ever seen them now that her walls are down and her secret is out. Sophia leans forward, brushing her lips against mine. "I couldn't until you showed me how."

Her mouth covers mine, and she swallows down my questions in an all-consuming kiss. Sophia locks her ankles behind my back and wraps her arms around my shoulders, clinging to me as I carry her out of the water and over to the pool house.

I've wanted her since the first moment I saw her, but I was waiting to be with her fully until she let me in. The brave, beautiful goddess in my arms is taking back control of her life, and I'm the lucky son of a bitch who gets to be with her every step of the way.

After shuffling my way inside, I untangle Sophia and set her on the ground, though I don't let her get very far. My hands slide up and down her curves while I kiss her soft, already swollen lips. She melts against me, her body becoming pliant as I kiss and touch and feel all of her, everything she is.

Sophia runs her hands up my torso and loops her arms around my neck, pulling me back down for a punishing kiss. I open up and take what she's offering, meeting each frantic stroke of her tongue with just as much passion and need as she's giving me.

She closes her eyes and tilts her head back, breaking our kiss so she can gulp down air. Her hands drift down to my biceps, where she grips me tightly, keeping me in place. I'm sure as fuck not going anywhere.

I can't keep my lips off her for one goddamn second. I kiss down her neck and lick the hollow of her throat before nipping the sensitive skin there. Sophia moans and digs her nails into my flesh, making me growl and grind my hard as fuck dick into her heat.

"Gonna lick up every drop of water from your sexy fucking body, Sophia. Then I'm gonna show you how amazing you are. How amazing I can make you feel."

Her eyes pop open, glowing with lust and hunger. Good. I plan to satisfy my woman on every level – carnal, physical, emotional, whatever the fuck she needs. She'll get it from *me* now.

She leans in at the same time I do, our lips crashing together as our need amplifies. Her desperate kiss mirrors my own, her eager hands clawing at me and begging me to give us what we both want. More.

I tear my mouth away from hers just long enough to peel her swimsuit top off, and then my lips are back on her skin, trailing down her neck. "Need to be inside you, love," I murmur into the shell of her ear. Sophia lets out a sexy, needy little whimper as I slip my hand into her swimsuit bottoms. My fingers part her folds and find her clit, massaging circles over the bundle of nerves. "Damn, you need it too, don't you?"

Her cunt is fucking drenched, and not from our time in the pool. I don't even have to ask if she's ready, but I want to hear her say it anyway.

"God yes, Aiden. I need you. Please, please, don't make me wait." Hearing her beg for me is sweeter than anything I've ever experienced. A wave of pleasure rushes down my spine, drawing my balls up tight and making precum leak out of me like a damn faucet. Fuck, this woman is my undoing.

I rid her of the last remaining scrap of fabric, then lift her up into my arms, carrying my incredible woman to bed. I toss her on the mattress and then strip down, adrenaline pumping in my veins and urging me to claim her right the fuck now.

Sophia is spread out for me on the bed, her chocolatey hair a tangled mess, her swollen lips slightly parted, her chest heaving with shallow breaths. Goddamn, she's gorgeous. And *mine.* She's all mine.

I climb onto the bed and crawl up her body, kissing her thighs, torso, breasts, neck, and finally, her sweet lips. I rub my body against hers, needing that friction, needing to feel her skin against mine, needing to prove she's really here and that tragedy didn't take her from me before I had the chance to make her mine.

"I'm right here," she whispers, cupping my cheek. I stare into her hazel eyes, not even questioning how she read my mind. She knows me, sees me, understands me in a way no one else ever has.

I nod and take a breath, centering myself once more. Sophia presses her lips to mine, her tongue seeking entrance. I give my girl everything she wants, opening my mouth to welcome her kiss.

It starts off slow, with tentative licks. I groan at her innocence but manage not to take control. Yet. Sophia explores my mouth, then pulls my bottom lip through her teeth, making me growl. She grins mischievously at me, and fuck, it physically pains me to hold back my orgasm. Shit, this can't be over before it even began.

"You like knowing you have control over me, love?"

"Mmhm," she nods, her lip twisting into a flirty smile.

Sophia gasps and then giggles as I flip our positions so she's on top. "Then take it, baby. Take control."

She braces herself on my chest, pushing herself up and adjusting to our new position. I slide my hands up her thighs and squeeze, helping her rock against me. Sophia licks her damn lips as she rolls her hips, rubbing her pussy up and down my shaft. The head of my cock taps her clit and she shivers, repeating the motion.

I reach out and cup her tits, weighing them in my hands and brushing my thumbs over her nipples.

"Yes," she hisses out, her movements stuttering as she leans into my touch.

I play with her hardened peaks, twisting them and plucking them while Sophia claws at my chest and rubs against me, getting herself off without me even entering her. Fuck, it's so damn hot watching her get all worked up, knowing I have so much more in store for her.

Sophia's movements grow frantic as she writhes on top of me. I feel her cream dripping from her pussy, so close to coming already. A shiver runs down her spine and she holds her breath, preparing for her orgasm. I feel it pushing forward, demanding to be felt, making her whimper with each breath.

Right before it takes her under, I grip her hips and hold her still. Sophia looks down at me with confusion and frustration but then understanding dawns on her when I line myself up with her entrance. I groan when I feel her tight little channel pulse around the head of my cock. Goddamn, her greedy little pussy is trying to suck me inside.

"Ready for me, Sophia? Ready to be mine?" She nods, her hazel eyes glossed over with lust as she circles her hips, trying to get me where she wants me. I hold her in place above me, not giving in just yet. "I need your words, baby. Tell me how much you want this."

"I've wanted you for as long as I knew what it meant to be with someone like this," she whispers. "I've never wanted anyone else. I've never..." Sophia looks away from me as a pink blush creeps into her cheeks.

My heart stills in my chest. No way. I need her to tell me. I need her to say the words. "Never what, baby?"

"I've never..." She falters for a second, and then gains her confidence back, looking me right in the eyes. "I'm a virgin, Aiden. I've only ever wanted you, and I'm going to have you."

The determined look on her face along with the knowledge that I'm going to be her first and last, has me growling like a fucking beast. She shocks the hell out of me by growling back and then slamming her tight as fuck pussy down on my cock.

"Jesus fuck!" I roar, holding her still when she's fully seated. Sophia whimpers and I lean up to kiss her pain away. "You did so good, love," I say, trying to make my voice soothing even though the most intense pressure is building up inside me, ready to take over and fuck my woman properly. "Take it slow, we have forever."

She nods and kisses me again, her tense body relaxing ever so much as I run my hands up and down her thighs and back. I grip her ass and help her rock against me and circle her hips, finding what feels good.

"Yes!" Sophia cries out, wiggling her hips and hitting her G-spot against my thick dick. She shudders and moans, rolling her sexy fucking body on top of mine, totally taking control of her pleasure.

I cup her breast and pinch her nipple, groaning when more of her cream spills out. Jesus, I barely manage to keep it together when I look down and see where we're connected. Watching her tight, wet little cunt stretch obscenely wide to take in my many inches is something I'll remember for the rest of my life.

"That's it, Sophia. That's so fucking it," I growl, moving both of my hands to her hips, jerking her up and down as I meet her thrust for thrust. Her pussy flutters around me as her muscles lock up tight.

Sophia rolls forward, resting her hands on either side of my head. Her lips find mine and we kiss and fuck like the world's on fire. She buries her face into the side of my neck and sobs as her body shakes and tightens around me. My beautiful woman bites my neck and creams all over my cock as she reaches her climax.

Feeling her orgasm absolutely devastate her snaps something inside of me.

I roll over, changing our position and fucking into that little pussy, unable to control myself. Her back bows off the bed and her legs wrap around me, holding me close. She digs her heels into my ass and claws my back, leaving her mark on me as another orgasm rattles through her.

"So good, baby," I growl, before claiming her lips as my own.

I devour her, biting at her lips and spearing my tongue inside of her eager mouth, licking up every inch and then sucking on her tongue. It's a wild, messy kiss, one that matches the way I'm fucking her like a goddamn animal.

I slide one hand down her body and grip her ass cheek, changing the angle of her hips and helping her meet me thrust for thrust. My cock scrapes against her most sensitive spot with each fierce stroke.

She's breaking apart for me; I can feel it. Every time I hit the end of her, she cracks a little more, the pressure of her orgasm building and pulsing and pushing her boundaries.

My balls draw up tight as my own orgasm gathers in the base of my spine. My rhythm falters slightly as I try to hold on, needing her to come with me. "Get there, baby, fuck, please get there. Need one more from you."

"It's too much, too much, I'm scared..."

"I've got you, Sophia. Let go for me, I'm right here. Let go, love. Come for me."

She sucks in a huge breath and holds it, her entire body trembling, and then freezing. Every damn muscle is pulled so tight as she clings to me with everything she has. With one last brutal thrust, we both shatter completely.

Sophia floods my cock with her release, and I give her everything in return, my cum splashing into her throbbing pussy as she sucks in every last drop. We're both grunting, shaking, and sweating as we ride that high together.

Eventually, she goes limp in my arms. I bury my face into the side of her neck and pump into her twice more before collapsing. I roll to the side and drape my freshly fucked little angel over my chest.

"Holy shit," she mumbles into my chest, her voice all scratchy as she catches her breath.

"Yeah," I agree, just as worn out and in awe as she is. I mean...fuck. If I didn't know before, I definitely know now – she's it for me. "Are you okay?" Doubt and worry rush in to take the place of euphoria. "I was so rough with—"

Sophia cuts me off with a kiss. "You were perfect," she whispers into my lips before kissing me again. "Absolutely perfect. I can't wait to do it again."

I curse under my breath and tangle my fingers in her hair, angling her head to deepen our kiss. My cock is sore from how hard I fucked her, but damn if he isn't twitching to life, ready for another round.

There's something I need to tell her first, though. Something I should have told her before I took her virginity, or rather, before she gave her virginity to me. My girl knew exactly what she wanted, and hell if that wasn't the sexiest damn thing in the world.

"Sophia," I murmur, cupping the side of her face and drawing it up so I can look at her. "I lo—"

The sound of glass breaking shatters our tender moment. I'm up in a flash, worried that Josiah saw us together and lost his shit.

"Stay here," I tell Sophia as I look around the small bedroom for something to wear. All I had on were my swim trunks. She points to the closet and tells me Josiah has some of his old clothes in there. I quickly throw on a shirt and some sweatpants and head out to the main room.

It's not Josiah standing there looking angry as hell.

Shit. How am I going to explain this to Sophia?

Chapter 10

Sophia

I know Aiden told me to stay here, but like hell I'm going to let him face Josiah alone. I know that's who is out there. Who else would it be? I figure going out there with a sheet wrapped around me isn't the best idea, so I rummage through my dresser and finally find shorts and a T-shirt.

I start talking before I've even rounded the corner to the main room, hoping to deescalate the situation before he breaks something else. Then again, it's his property, he can do what he wants.

"Josiah, we're together and there's nothing you can—"

"And *who* the fuck is *she*?!" A stick thin, blonde woman wearing a sequined cocktail dress points at me, stabbing the air with her long, fake nail. "Are you *cheating* on me? After all we've been through?" the woman screeches.

I'm stunned as I take in the scene. Frozen in place. I can't move or speak as I look at the lounge chair this chick must have thrown through the sliding glass door to get in. Cheating? Am I the other woman?

I look to Aiden, waiting for him to deny their relationship and call her crazy. Instead, he looks like he's debating what to say. Like he knows he's stuck in an impossible position and he's going to piss off one of the women in this room. My heart sinks to my stomach as big fat tears well up in my eyes. I'm not pissed. I'm heartbroken.

"Sophia..." Aiden says, taking a step closer to me.

"Don't you talk to her! Don't even look at her! How could you?"

"Trinity, has it really been you this whole time?" Aiden turns away from me, taking the last piece of my broken heart along with him. I don't know what he's talking about, but I don't want the details. As soon as I can move my feet again, I'm out of here.

"Of course. We were always meant to be together. Don't you see that now? Don't you see the lengths I would go to, for you to be mine?"

My stomach rolls at her words, bile burning the back of my throat. Is this the real reason Aiden returned to Texas? To get away from an ex? Oh my God, am I the rebound girl? Is he about to get back together with this Trinity person?

Aiden sneaks a glance at me, his face completely unreadable. I feel the walls closing in on me, the familiar suffocating pressure seizing my lungs.

"*I said don't look at her*!" Trinity screams, making Aiden jump and snap his head in her direction. Something about that frees me from my frozen state.

I run to the bedroom and begin throwing clothes into a suitcase. I'm not sure where I'm going, but I need some space. I can hardly take a full breath, let alone think clearly enough about everything that just happened.

"Trinity, calm down. You found me, alright? Let's not make a bigger scene," I hear Aiden say. I hate his soothing voice when it's directed at her.

"I'm sorry," the woman bursts into theatrical tears. "I just missed you so much. I was worried when I didn't see you around, especially after my last note."

"Let's get out of here, yeah? We can talk about us."

I can't stop the tears from spilling over my cheeks, but I manage to plant my face into the mattress in time to muffle my sobs. He's really just leaving with her? No explanation or even a second glance?

Part of me still can't accept what's happening. He couldn't have faked the way he held me in the pool while I cried in his arms or the way he understood me and my need to capture my trauma on canvas. And yet, when I poke my head out of the bedroom, I see him and Trinity walk outside, arm in arm. How could I have been so wrong about him?

***

An hour later, I find myself in my old bedroom at my parents' house. Yes, this is a new low for me. Despite my mom and dad kicking me out when

I didn't go back to college, they aren't totally heartless. When I called my mom in tears, asking for a place to stay for the night, she said my room was ready for me and she and my dad would be working late. At least some things never change.

I sent Josiah a text as soon as I left the house, letting him know I'm staying with mom and dad for the night. I figure Aiden can explain the broken glass door when he gets back from wherever he took Trinity. My brother called right away, wanting to know about my change of heart. I honestly can't remember what excuse I told him, but after a few minutes, he seemed satisfied.

I dig around my closet and find a sketchpad, hoping to process the events of the day through my art, but the lines are all wrong. Everything is wrong. Not being with Aiden after he made love to me is wrong. Knowing he left with another woman is wrong. Mooching off my brother while I pout and paint is wrong.

It's time for a change. A big one. I know I'm acting irrationally, but fuck it, nothing else in life seems to be panning out the way I thought, so why not try doing things a different way?

I pull out my phone and start scrolling through the internship emails my mom has been blasting me with. One in particular catches my eye. It's an internship for a firm in Boston that's looking for someone to add to their audit team. I may not want to be a part of the business world, but the idea of starting over somewhere new is tempting. Too tempting.

Without overthinking it, I call my mom, knowing she'll be more than willing to set it up for me. A few minutes after we hang up, my phone dings with a text from my mom, confirming my internship and the flight info for tomorrow morning. Good lord, that woman works fast.

I take a deep breath and scroll through my contacts until I get to Aiden's name. My thumb hovers over the delete button for a few seconds before I press down. Contact deleted. Connection severed. Heart shattered.

Chapter 11

Aiden

Holy fuck, I'm exhausted. After letting Trinity take me to a coffee shop so we could "talk about us," I excused myself so I could make a few calls. Namely, to Josiah so he could report a break-in and vandalization, and then to Logan, to tell him I figured out who the stalker was.

I tried calling Sophia, too, but she didn't answer. I didn't expect her to after what just happened, but I had to try. Hopefully, she'll be more open to talking in person.

Trinity and I were in a movie together a few years ago. She had a minor role, something to do with a side character's friend or some shit like that. I'm used to women being obsessive and even aggressive on set, but no way did I think Trinity was capable of something like this. And what timing, too.

I was about to tell Sophia I love her when Trinity came bursting in, quite literally. She was the last person I expected to see, but one look at her wild eyes and deranged grimace, and I knew she'd been the one sending threatening letters and vandalizing my property.

The look Sophia gave me when she first saw Trinity nearly dropped me to my knees. She was beyond being hurt. I saw betrayal in her hazel eyes, along with a soul deep sadness. I hate that I made her feel that way, and I fucking loathe that Trinity forced my hand.

While Trinity was waving her arms around and yelling at me about Sophia, I saw the dark, shiny metal of a handgun poking out of her purse. She wasn't fucking around. Trinity came armed and ready to take me back to L.A. with her by any means necessary. No way in hell was I going to risk Sophia's safety, even if it meant being cold and cruel to her in the moment.

I know I have a lot of explaining to do, and a lot of groveling as well, but she has to know I'd never betray her like that, right? Then again, she's been through so much, even just in the last twenty-four hours. Jesus, was it just earlier this afternoon I held her in the pool while she worked through her fear? Was it really just a few hours ago that we made love? I took her damn virginity and then literally left with another woman. I didn't have a choice, but goddamnit, I hope Sophia will understand. She has to.

"You still there, Aiden?" Logan asks, his voice booming over the phone.

"Yeah," I mutter, trying to clear my thoughts enough to talk to my agent. Soon. Soon this will be over and I can get back to my Sophia.

"Everything squared away with the cops?"

"For the most part. Once they showed up to arrest Trinity at the coffee shop, she pretty much confessed to everything."

"Trinity," he snorts in disbelief. "Who would have thought? I'm sorry you had to find out this way."

"I know, man. It's not your fault," I sigh. The weight of the day sits heavy on my shoulders and sinks down into my chest. I ache to talk to Sophia about everything, but I needed to make sure Trinity was dealt with and thrown in jail before facing Sophia again.

"So, when are you coming back?" Logan asks.

"Uh..."

Logan groans over the phone, already bracing himself for bad news. "What's keeping you there?"

"The love of my life," I answer immediately.

"The fuck you talking about?"

"Sophia Turner. Josiah's little sister." Damn, that reminds me I really need to talk to him. My confession is met with silence, so I continue. "She's it for me, and nothing you can say will stop me from making her mine."

After another stretch of silence, Logan finally responds. "I'm not trying to keep you from happiness, Aiden. If you say she's the one, then I believe you."

"Really?"

"Of course. I know I can be controlling and opinionated, but I really do have your best interests at heart."

"Does that mean you'll stop dismissing my screenplay?"

"Yeah," he sighs. "I'm sorry I got carried away with forcing acting jobs down your throat. I'll still have an opinion on your choices, and I can't promise I won't be controlling from time to time, but it's your life and your career. I can respect that."

"That was...unexpected, but thank you."

Logan grumbles something in acknowledgment, clearly done with the emotional confessions for the day. I agree to call him tomorrow when everything is settled with Trinity.

I sit in my parked rental car outside Josiah's house, gathering my thoughts before heading inside. It's been six long hours away from my Sophia, and that is unacceptable.

"Aiden, glad you're back," Josiah greets me when I walk in the front door. "After I gave my statement and pressed charges, the cops told me they had more questions for you and I should go home."

I nod absentmindedly while looking around for my woman. "Is Sophia okay?"

"Yeah, she's at our parents' house."

"What?"

"Sophia texted me earlier today and said she's spending the night with our parents. It was right before you called about the break-in. She must have left just before anything happened, thank God."

"She's with your mom and dad?" I ask, completely perplexed.

Josiah nods. "Apparently, she wants to try and reconcile," he shrugs.

"Oh." I don't know what to say to that. Shit, I did a lot more damage than I thought if I sent her right back to her cold parents who don't understand or appreciate her. "I'm going to start cleaning up the mess Trinity left behind," I say, excusing myself to the pool house. It's not just the broken glass I need to take care of. I need to take care of my Sophia and her broken heart.

***

It's official. I'm a miserable, pathetic fucking mess. I tried calling and texting at least twenty times last night, but Sophia is ignoring me. I don't blame her, but I need to fucking see her and make this right. It's nine in the morning now, and I decide it's just as good a time as any to roll my sorry ass out of bed. I need to figure out a way to get my woman back.

I half expect to see Sophia sitting at the table, but of course, she's not there. Instead, Josiah is at the table, sipping his coffee.

"Morning," I say, while pouring a cup of coffee for myself.

"Hey," he says distractedly while scrolling through his phone. Josiah has a confused, concerned look on his face as he reads and rereads whatever is on the screen.

"Everything okay?"

"Uh...yeah. I just got some...interesting news."

"Oh?"

"Sophia took an internship in Boston. She flew out early this morning."

"What?!" I roar, dropping my mug of hot coffee. I hardly feel the scalding liquid splash over my bare feet. The mug shatters, but I barely even hear it over the sound of blood rushing through my ears, making me lightheaded.

"What the hell, Aiden?" Josiah says, getting up from the table.

"I love her," I blurt out. I'm shaking with fear, anger, hurt, and helplessness. I don't have time to ease Josiah into this, he needs to know right here, right fucking now, so he can help me get her back.

Silence fills the kitchen as we stare at each other. I know I look like a wreck. That's because I am. Completely wrecked.

"You love her," Josiah repeats slowly, never breaking eye contact. "Do you even know her? Do you know what she's been through this last year?"

"Yes, I love her. And yes, she told me about almost...fuck, I can't even think about it. Why didn't you tell me?"

He looks shocked by my anger, but he quickly recovers. "It's not like you two were close growing up. And Sophia is so private, especially about the accident."

"I...I love her," I say again, trying to find the words to convince her protective older brother I'm not just fucking around.

"Back up. What *actually* happened yesterday?" Josiah doesn't look mad, per se, which I'm counting as a win.

"We were, uh...together in the pool house when Trinity broke in."

"Fuck," he mutters, wiping a hand down his face.

"Yeah. She doesn't know the whole story. I had to get Trinity away from her. There wasn't any time to explain. Please tell me how I can find her. Where is she staying in Boston? What is she doing for her internship? You have to believe me, Josiah, I love her so goddamn much. It's killing me that she thinks I betrayed her."

"Well, shit," he sighs. "You sure look messed up enough to be in love. If I tell you how to find her, will you promise not to fuck things up again? I mean it, Sophia has been through the wringer, and the last thing she needs is some dude toying with her heart."

"I'm not some dude," I growl. "I'm her future husband." Josiah's eyebrows lift up, nearly to his hairline. Yeah, I said it. I'm all in, and he needs to know it. "Look, you know me," I say in a more human voice, though it's still a bit rough. "I'm not some player or Hollywood bad boy. I don't think I even want to act anymore. That's part of what this whole break from my life was about. Finding my inspiration again."

"Did you find it?"

"I found so much more. I found my muse. The love of my life. My leading lady."

Josiah groans and makes a gagging sound. "That was cheesy as fuck." I shrug, not even caring about his judgment. I meant every word. He eyes me up and down, and then comes to a decision. "Fine. But it goes without saying, I'll beat your ass if you break her heart, movie star or not."

"I wouldn't have it any other way."

Chapter 12

Sophia

If I had to choose a color to represent the Gray, Gray & Gray Accounting Firm, it'd be just that – gray. I seriously can't make this stuff up. The name is Gray, the carpet is gray, the metal filing cabinets lining the wall next to my cubical are gray, even the lady sharing the cubicle with me is wearing gray heels and a gray dress. To be fair, the walls are a bold *light* gray in color.

My mom booked me the earliest flight available, apparently wanting to get my ass out the door before I could second guess my decision to take the internship. I barely had time to drop my stuff off at the hotel before my phone rang. It was my new boss, requesting I come in at my earliest convenience to fill out the paperwork.

Looking around the colorless office space, I remind myself I'm not here to further my career, despite what my parents think. I'm here to start over. Once the internship is done, I'll figure out my next move.

My aching heart is confused about the whole thing, however. Whenever I think about big life choices, the first thing that pops into my head in Aiden. His silver-blue eyes, the slight stubble he let grow out while staying with us, his dark, perfectly messy, yet styled hair. And then there's his smile. His kiss...

Crap. I should *not* be thinking about Aiden, and I *definitely* shouldn't be thinking about the way his lips trailed down my body until he reached my...

"Oh my God, is that...?"

"No way!"

"Yeah, I think it is!"

My thoughts are disrupted by the hushed voices and excited, whispered words of my co-workers. I don't know anyone here, so I'm not interested in whomever just walked in.

"What would *he* be doing *here*?" The chatter grows louder as speculations are thrown around.

"Oh my God, oh my God, oh my God, he's coming this way," Andrea, my cubical mate, squeals.

The frenzied whispers die down instantly, and I feel a presence behind me. Not just any presence, though. It's a protective, possessive presence with a hint of sandalwood and citrus. It's Aiden Steele.

"Sophia." His deep, velvety voice rings out in the now deathly quiet office. "Look at me, love."

I dart my eyes over to Andrea, who is staring at me slack-jawed. She widens her eyes and tips her head in Aiden's direction as if to say, "Look at the movie star who is calling you by name, you idiot!" Her words, not mine.

I sigh, but before I get the chance to swivel in my chair, I feel a pair of strong, warm hands rest on my shoulders and spin me around. I'm not prepared to see Aiden again. I'm not prepared for the look of absolute remorse, longing, and brokenness in his eyes. You'd think we hadn't seen each other in years instead of a handful of hours with the way he's looking at me right now.

"Sophia," he says again, reaching out to catch a tear I didn't realize had escaped. Aiden surprises me by kneeling in front of me while I'm still sitting in my chair. He rests his hands on my thighs and looks up at me, pleading with me to hear whatever he's going to say next. "I know you're hurting, and I'm so fucking sorry I caused you any pain. I didn't have a choice. I had to protect you. Remember I told you I had a stalker?"

I furrow my brow in confusion, but then something clicks. "Trinity," I whisper.

Relief floods his eyes. I can see it washing over his whole body as Aiden's tense muscles relax ever so slightly. "She had a gun. I had to get her away from you. God, if anything ever happened to you, Sophia..." Aiden closes his eyes and his brow scrunches up, as if he's in physical pain. "If you got hurt because of me, I would never forgive myself. I love you too much to ever put you in danger. I love you so fucking much it hurts. I've been miserable without you."

He loves me. Aiden Steele loves me. I see it. Every look, every touch, everything he's said to me since coming back to our hometown...they were all done out of love. Even when he was cruel to me, it was to protect me. I sniffle and remove my hand from his to wipe more of my tears away. Aiden halts my movement, instead reaching up to do it himself.

"I made you cry. These tears are because of me, so it's my job to take them away," he murmurs. "Please forgive me, Sophia. Please believe me when I say I've never been in a relationship with Trinity. She became obsessed with me when she was an extra on a film I worked on a while ago. I had no idea how obsessed until yesterday."

Aiden is cupping my face now, trying to keep up with my steady stream of tears. He wasn't using me, he wanted to protect me this whole time. That sounds much more like the Aiden I've come to know.

"I'm sorry," I stutter out, launching myself into his arms. He catches me easily and wraps me up in his embrace.

"What for, baby? You didn't do anything wrong."

"I ran away from you. I didn't give you a chance to explain. I gave up on us before we even figured out what our relationship is. I mean, am I your girlfriend?"

"I was hoping you'd be my wife," he says, cupping my chin so I have to make eye contact. He's completely serious.

"Aiden," I whisper. "What about my brother?"

"How do you think I found you?" he says with a grin. My eyes go wide, but Aiden just winks at me. "And you didn't give up on us. You can't. I won't let you. Soon you'll be mine in every way. All you have to do is say yes."

He fumbles around in his pocket for something and then pulls out a small blue box. We're surrounded by gasps and excited whispers. I totally forgot Aiden and I are in an office full of nosey people.

"Do you really want to do this here?" I whisper, tilting my head toward our ever-growing audience. "Some of them are recording us!"

Aiden grins. "Then you better get your line right, love. I just need one word from you." He opens the box to reveal a gorgeous ring, not too gaudy, but stunning all the same. "I didn't know how unhappy I was until you brought true joy into my life. I didn't know how unsettled I was until you smiled at me the very first time and calmed me down. I didn't know how lonely I was until I tasted your lips. They felt like home."

"Home," I whisper, nodding my agreement.

"Sophia Turner, will you ma—"

"Yes!" I practically shout, throwing my arms around his neck and kissing the rest of his words from his mouth.

"You got the line right, but your timing was a bit off," Aiden chuckles once we break the kiss. The entire office breaks out in applause, and I bury my beet red face into the side of Aiden's neck. "Better get used to it, baby. The whole world is gonna know you're my girl soon. My wife. My everything."

I nod into the side of his neck, then kiss him there before lifting my head up. "I love you, Aiden Steele," I whisper into his lips before kissing him again.

It starts off sweet, like the beginning of a love story. But then he deepens it, letting me know our love is stronger now, more durable. It's everlasting. His kiss says it all.

Finally, he tears his mouth away from mine. "How much do you want to keep this internship?" he asks, his voice all husky as he tries to catch his breath.

"Not even a little bit," I grin. "I haven't even finished the paperwork for HR."

Aiden stands, with me still in his arms, and heads toward the door. "Wait! My—"

"Here," Andrea says, coming over to us and handing me my purse and coat. "That was so beautiful," she whispers, sniffling a bit and tearing up.

"Yeah, she is," Aiden says, kissing my temple.

I take one last look at the Gray, Gray & Gray ultra-gray office, then turn my gaze up toward my Aiden. He smiles down at me with all the love and devotion in the world. I know I'm looking at him the exact same way.

"What now?" I ask once we're in the elevator. Aiden still has me in his arms, and I'm not complaining one bit.

"Now, my sweet Sophia, I take you back to your hotel and make up for the last twenty-four hours," he whispers against my ear.

"Yes, please," I nod eagerly, grinning up at him.

***

We barely make it inside the hotel room before Aiden has my back pressed up against the wall, his tongue down my throat, and his hands roaming over my curves, clawing at my clothes. He pulls me away from the wall and somehow shuffles us toward the bed while stripping both of us down. We stand in front of each other for a moment, both of us bare, vulnerable, and yet completely seen and understood.

Aiden takes a step closer to me, erasing the distance between us. He runs his hands up and down my naked body, caressing my hips, my breasts, even my throat and lips. His strong, capable hands leave a throbbing, warm blaze in their wake.

His hand wraps around the back of my neck, pulling me into him for a punishing kiss. I'm his. He owns every part of me. That's what he's telling me with each stroke of his tongue, each anguished groan that travels through his body and into mine. I feel his kiss everywhere, and I need more.

Aiden guides me backward until the edge of the mattress hits the back of my legs. He gently lays me out on the bed, then stands in front of me, looking down at my body. It's all for him. I spread my legs, moaning when he growls and clenches his fists.

"Fuck, Sophia. You're so damn sexy." He's on me in the next instant, covering my body with openmouthed kisses, sucking on my skin, and leaving little love bites up my torso and on my breasts.

I jerk and twist beneath him, gasping for air and whimpering with each lingering touch and kiss. When he finally reaches my mouth, Aiden slants his lips over mine and leads us in a slow, drugging kiss.

My legs automatically spread wider so he can settle between them. I feel his long, thick cock glide against my pussy, collecting my juices and driving me crazy. He's *so close* to where I need him, I nearly cry in frustration.

Aiden sits back slightly and gathers my wrists up in one of his large hands, pinning them to the mattress before nuzzling into the side of my neck.

"Fuckin' love seeing you stretched out for me," he says into my skin, his voice low, gravelly, and desperate. Aiden drags his lips down my neck and across my collarbone, then he nips at the tops of my breasts, grinning wickedly when I jump and gasp. "Gonna fuck this sweet little pussy now, Sophia. Are you ready for me?"

I nod and tilt my hips, nudging the swollen head of his cock against my entrance. Aiden growls and reaches down between us to guide himself inside in one smooth stroke. Fire spreads through my veins, and heat pulses out from my core, overwhelming my body.

I wiggle my hips, making sparks sizzle and burn across my skin. Aiden groans, leaning over me, one hand still holding my wrists above my head while the other trails up my side. He squeezes my breast, pinching my hardened, sensitive nipple before sucking it into his mouth.

My back bows off the bed, and he takes the opportunity to slip his hand between my back and the mattress, pushing my chest up so he can feast on me. Aiden grinds his cock into me, filling me up before pulling back and slamming into me roughly.

My breasts jiggle with every thrust as he sets a relentless pace. I wrap my legs around him and dig my heels into his sculpted ass, crying out when he hits the spot inside me that pushes me right up to the edge.

I feel my muscles tense as my pussy tightens around his thickness. He lifts his head from my chest and studies my face, no doubt sensing how close I am. My thighs shake and a shiver runs up my spine, seizing my lungs and forcing out a scream as I come around his cock.

Rivulets of pleasure course through my body, making every nerve ending spark to life. Aiden fucks me through it, never letting up. He still has my wrists secured in his grasp, despite all my writhing around and trying to twist away from the intense pressure and sharp ecstasy he's creating deep inside me.

I swear I'm about to come again, but suddenly Aiden isn't on top of me anymore. I hardly have time to register his absence before his big hands grasp my hips firmly. Aiden flips me over effortlessly, then pulls my hips back so I'm on all fours.

"Fuck yes," he grunts, gripping my ass cheeks and spreading them wide. "Jesus Christ, I've pictured you like this too many damn times."

Aiden thrusts into me, growling when he bottoms out. I let out a broken cry as I unravel for him, my orgasm ricocheting through my body but never leaving me completely. I'm so fucking sensitive, so raw as he pounds into me.

"I-I-I ca-ca-n't..." I stutter out, unable to take a full breath.

"You can, baby. Trust me, you can. Feel this with me. *Fuck*, feel it, Sophia."

I whimper and nod my head, staying right here with him in the moment, struggling to hold myself up on shaky arms while my pussy knots around him over and over. Incoherent words and strangled, almost tormented sounds fall from my lips as Aiden tears me apart, fucks me so good, so hard, so damn rough. He's branding me with each savage stroke, claiming all of me, body and soul.

My fingers curl into the sheets, fisting them as I try desperately to hold myself up. When he brushes the tips of his fingers over my clit, my knees wobble and my arms give out completely. I face plant into the pillow, my ass still in the air, Aiden still pounding away. He pinches my clit and I sob out yet another orgasm. My pleasure spikes as white-hot bliss fills my veins. When it fades away, I'm completely limp. Boneless. Held up only by Aiden's punishing grip on my hips.

Aiden lets out a feral roar as his cum fills me up. He pulls back and then enters me again as more of his release shoots out of him. There's so much, I feel it dripping down my thighs, the tickling sensation making me moan and involuntarily tremble in his arms.

I feel the last of his orgasm drain from him, and then Aiden collapses on top of me. He's sweaty and panting for air as he rests his forehead between my shoulder blades. I feel his hot breath on my skin, the weight of his body on top of mine, his sweat mixing with mine, and I know.

I just...know.

Everything will work out as long as we're together. Whether in L.A., Texas, or a different country entirely, it doesn't matter. My parents' disapproval doesn't matter. All the other obstacles that will get in our way, all the people who might not understand, or try to tear us apart...they just don't matter. *This* is what matters. Right here.

Aiden rolls off me and pulls me into his arms, draping my still boneless body across his chest. We don't say anything, and we don't need to. Aiden combs his fingers through my hair and kisses the top of my head, his breathing finally returning to normal.

"I know we have some big decisions to make soon, but I don't care where we end up or what we do, as long as you're mine," he murmurs, echoing my thoughts.

I tilt my head up and smile, getting lost in his loving gaze. Those blue eyes of his with flecks of silver get me every time. "I'm yours," I whisper, brushing my lips against his.

"And I'm yours, Sophia. So fucking yours."

Aiden seals his declaration with the kind of kiss you only see in movies. This ain't no Hollywood blockbuster, though. It's my real life, and for the first time in forever, I think I just might get my happily ever after.

Epilogue

Aiden

I watch my beautiful wife adjust one of her paintings and stand back to make sure it's straight. It's her first gallery exhibit and she's been stressing out about it for weeks. I know she's going to be amazing and this is just the start of her career as an artist.

My gorgeous Sophia huffs out a breath and puts her fists on her hips, staring at the painting in question. I walk up behind her and slip my arms around her waist, pulling her back to my front. I press a soft kiss to the side of her neck, smiling to myself when she relaxes and leans into me.

"Everything is perfect, love," I murmur, my lips ghosting over the shell of her ear.

Sophia sighs and melts against me completely, surrendering to my care for her. I close my eyes and tighten my hold on her, letting her know without words that I'll always be here to comfort and support her. God, I'll never take her trust in me for granted.

It's been six months since I proposed and brought Sophia home with me. We got married as soon as possible, neither one of us willing to wait a second longer than necessary to start the rest of our lives together.

"Thanks," Sophia whispers, turning her head to kiss my cheek.

"Just remember to take deep breaths and let me know if you start to feel suffocated, okay, baby?"

She nods her head, taking a deep breath. We stand there, looking at her painting, both of us getting lost in the emotion she brought out onto the canvas. I look around at her other pieces, taking in everything as I hold her close.

There are her early works from right after the incident. Dark, blurry, and somehow suffocating when you look at them. These are from the depths of the water, the depths of despair. Then the fog clears, and her next set of paintings are blurry, like the first one I saw the day I startled her in the pool house.

The next set of paintings are from a different angle completely, looking down at the water. There's such depth there. You can still see the blackness in the very deepest parts, as well as the blurred ripples of the water, but the majority of the paintings are bright and clear. Like my Sophia. She's grown so much.

I encouraged her to start therapy – something her parents had previously scoffed at – and it's helped her process her trauma in a healthy way. I'm so damn proud of all the hard work she's doing, and I can't believe I get to be the one to see her grow and achieve all her dreams.

I hear the clicking of heels on the hardwood floor and turn to see the gallery director coming our way.

"Showtime, love," I whisper, kissing her temple and reluctantly stepping away from her.

I watch my wife shake hands and charm everyone who walks through the door. The gallery fills up with more and more people seeing and adoring my talented wife's artwork. She deserves every heartfelt compliment and awed praise.

Josiah arrives, along with their parents. He wraps Sophia up in a hug, the pride clear in his eyes. I walk over and shake everyone's hands, then tuck Sophia into my side, kissing the top of her head. She talks with her parents, who have since come around to her aspirations as an artist. Of course, they didn't change their minds until she booked the showing here at The Broad, one of the top galleries in the country.

Nevertheless, Sophia is making an effort to connect with her mom and dad again, though she's still cautious of their intentions. I certainly understand people wanting to use you for your money and fame, and I admire her so much for still wanting to have a relationship with her parents.

I see Logan walk in, and I excuse myself to go greet him. Ever since our heart-to-heart, we've settled into more of a friendship than a strictly agent/client relationship.

"Thanks for coming, Logan," I say, shaking his hand.

"I wouldn't miss it," he says with a smile. "Your girl is talented, that's for sure."

"Damn right she is." There's no hiding the pride in my voice.

"How's the screenplay coming along?"

I grin and shake my head. "I'm still not used to you asking about it," I chuckle. "But I'm close to finishing. You got any up and comers in mind for the roles? I don't want this to be a star-studded cast. I want new talent."

"As you've said about ten thousand times," Logan says, rolling his eyes. He grins a few seconds later, letting me know he's kidding.

We chat as people come and go, but eventually I can't stand to be away from my wife a single second longer. When the crowd finally starts to die down, I pull her into a secluded hallway and cup the back of her neck, leaning down to taste her sweet lips.

"I'm so proud of you," I whisper into her open mouth before kissing her again. "You were amazing tonight."

I continue pressing light, teasing kisses up and down her neck, slowly guiding her backward until she's pressed up against the wall. My hands slide down her soft curves, then rest on her round, juicy ass. I give it a squeeze and pull her closer as my lips meet hers once again.

"Are you trying to seduce me, Mr. Steele?" Sophia asks. I swallow down her words with a deep, demanding kiss.

"Always, Mrs. Steele. I'll be seducing you for the rest of our lives."

My Sophia smiles up at me, her hazel eyes shining with pure love and adoration. "I like the sound of that."

"Me too, baby. Me fucking too."

I take her hand in mine and lead her back toward the gallery. Toward the rest of our lives. Toward our happily ever after.

Don't miss out!

Visit the website below and you can sign up to receive emails whenever Cameron Hart publishes a new book. There's no charge and no obligation.

https://books2read.com/r/B-A-STTM-ETTNC

BOOKS 2 READ

Connecting independent readers to independent writers.

About the Author

Hello. I'm Cameron Hart, and I write sweet steamy romances. I'm a *USA Today* Bestselling author with over forty books available. I write romance with lots of heat, plenty of sweet, and just enough drama to keep things interesting. I graduated from the Iowa Writer's Workshop in 2012 with a degree in creative writing. When I'm not working on my next book, I can be found reading, crocheting, doing yoga, and chasing around my grumpy cats.

What to expect from a Cameron Hart book: Lots of heat, plenty of sweet, and just enough drama to keep things interesting. No cheating, safe, guaranteed HEA!

Read more at https://cameronhart.net/.